SECRET HISTORY

DRAGON WORLD

S. A. CALDWELL

CARLTON
BOOKS

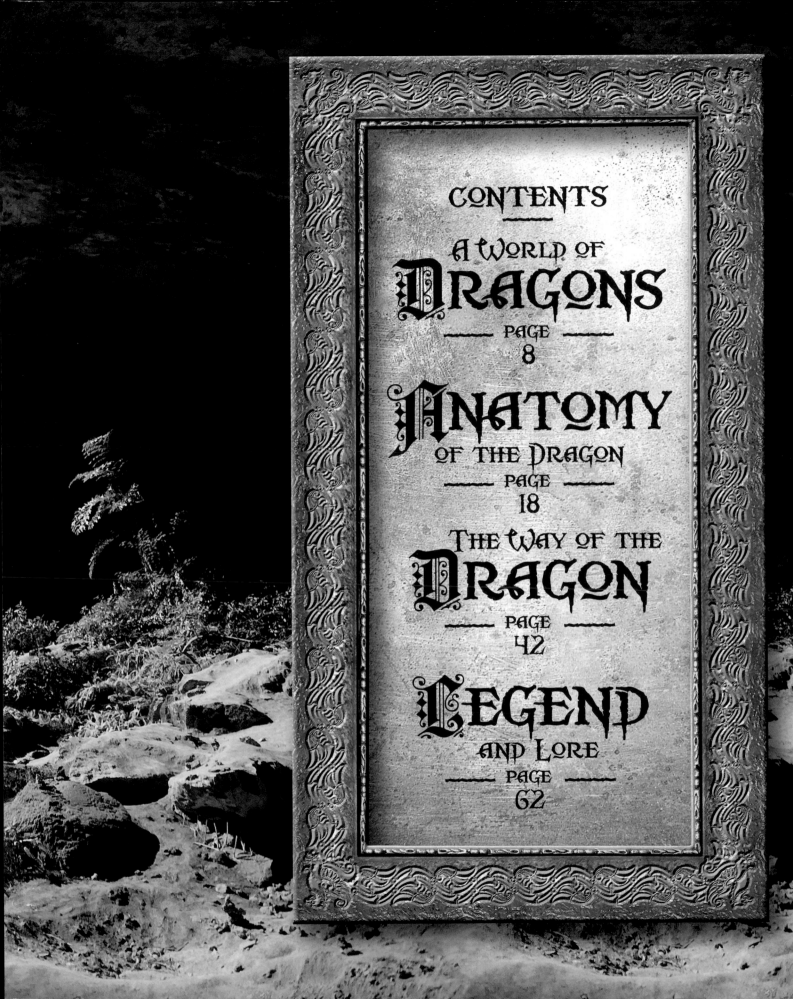

CONTENTS

DRAGONS ARE EVERYWHERE.

THEY ARE THE ROARING OF THE WIND, A FLICKER IN THE NIGHT SKY, A RUSTLING IN THE FOREST. THEY ARE THE GLINT BENEATH A DESERT SUN, A STIRRING IN STILL WATERS, THE FURY IN THE EYE OF A STORM.

THROUGHOUT THE AGES, man has sought to understand and tame the mighty dragon. So few have seen this extraordinary animal, yet all know his name. These creatures inhabit every part of our world, and yet remain as elusive and mysterious as ever. What exactly is this fabulous beast we call the dragon?

This is the question that has long burned in my heart. The book you hold in your hands is a labour of love, the fruit of a lifetime's enquiry. Within it you will find a series of observations, the result of many years of research. My quest has taken me to some of Earth's remotest places - to vast mountain ranges and immense, silent deserts; to dark, ancient forests and desolate, frozen landscapes. And yet the greatest challenge of all has been to open the mind to unthought-of possibilities, for dragons defy the ordinary. As you turn these pages, be prepared to embrace the unknown, to expect the incredible, to see with unworldly eyes.

Perhaps most dramatic of all for the reader are the astonishing collections displayed here for the first time ever. One can only marvel at the Drachenfels teeth, buried for close to a thousand years in ancient castle ruins before their chance discovery, or the magnificent claw specimens gathered from the far-flung corners of the world. Many have warned of the perils in seeking to possess any part of a dragon. The individuals who create these extraordinary collections risk all in their desire to further the study of this beast. We owe them much.

No man can ever hope to know the dragon. So it has always been, and so it will remain. But it is my best wish that these pages bring you a little closer to understanding something of the powerful allure that defines these strange and wonderful creatures.

S. A. CALDWELL
The Ancient Guild of Dragon Research

A WORLD OF DRAGONS

Dragons can be found across the far reaches of our world. They are masters of the skies, soaring majestically over vast and scorching deserts or snowy, frozen lands. They swoop down from glittering mountain peaks in a blaze of fire and rise up from the bowels of the earth. Some slither serpent-like through rivers and lakes, ascending to the clouds in a flash of thunder, whilst others lurk unseen at the hearts of ancient forests.

As varied as the realms they inhabit, dragons have made this world their very own...

DRAGON REALMS
A STUDY OF HABITATS

Many dragon species skulk unseen just beneath the murky surfaces of swamps and marshes.

DRAGONS MAKE THEIR LAIRS in an astonishing range of places. Indeed, they can be divided into seven main types according to habitat: mountain, woodland and forest, savannah and prairie, freshwater, marsh and swamp, polar, and desert. A very few species are found in the world's oceans and seas, but most dragons are unable to thrive in salt water.

Rare dragons may be found in the most extreme environments. For example the Laki Lava Dragon of Iceland lives amongst the hot bubbling geysers, and is known to have survived lakes of molten lava.

DRAGON VARIETY

As with all Earth's creatures, it is fascinating to observe the ways in which dragons have adapted to live successfully in their particular habitats. Ice dragons with their almost translucent silvery scales blend seamlessly into snowy landscapes, whilst the nocturnal Flaming Humped Dragon of north Africa escapes the scorching desert sun by hiding away in its underground lair during daylight hours. The eyes, ears and nostrils of swamp dragons lie across the top of their heads - this allows them to lurk for many hours just beneath the surface of foul-smelling bogs, watching and waiting for tasty morsels to pass their way.

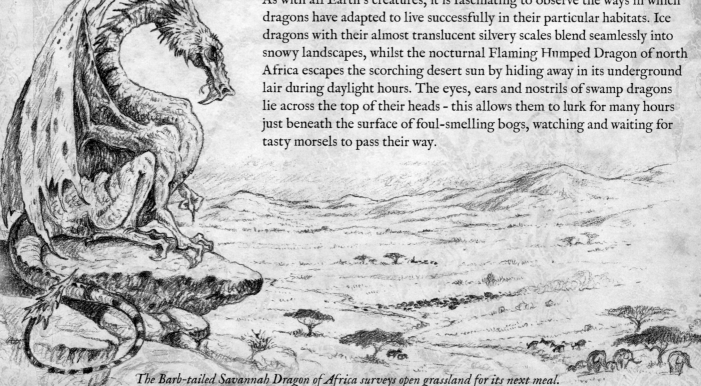

The Barb-tailed Savannah Dragon of Africa surveys open grassland for its next meal.

THE ROUGH MOUNTAIN TERRAIN OF THE SNAGGLE-TOOTHED MOUNTAIN DRAGON

*Mountain dragons are exceptionally agile and surefooted,
allowing them to clamber nimbly over steep rocks and rugged terrain.*

Glacier Cave of the Antarctic Snow Dragon

This magnificent creature has only rarely been seen by human eyes. Found at the heart of frozen Antarctica, it spends days at a time in its glacial lair during the long, harsh winter. When hungry, this dragon emerges to circle over the Antarctic sea, plunging into its icy depths to capture orcas and large seals.

Dragon Gallery
A Study of Species

So diverse and numerous are dragon species, that it would be impossible to name and describe them all on these pages. Shown here are six dragons from different habitats to represent the dazzling variety found amongst dragonkind.

The Snaggle-toothed Mountain Dragon makes its lair at high altitude in central and eastern Europe. Like all mountain species, this dragon has extraordinary eyesight, and is distinguished by a curious misalignment of its front teeth, which are nevertheless horribly vicious in attack.

The Razor-fanged Marsh Dragon is found principally in southern Asia and is an ever-present threat to passing birds, mammals such as deer and buffalo, and even humans. This species cannot fly, but is surprisingly nimble on dry land.

The Pygmy Forest Dragon

lives at the heart of America and Canada's temperate forests. Although no bigger than an antelope, this agile and muscular dragon includes bears and mountain lions in its diet.

The Crystal Ice Dragon

makes its home in the snowy polar lands. Pearl-like and almost translucent in appearance, this magnificent creature soars through the skies and breathes out blasts of icy air to stun its prey of polar bears, musk oxen and moose.

The Five-clawed Serpent Dragon

dwells in the rivers and lakes of eastern Asia. This species is wingless, but can rise to the clouds with the aid of a discreet lump on top of its head. Possessed with a remarkable intelligence, this dragon is known to transform into many guises.

The Triple-horned Night Dragon

is a relatively rare species found on the open rangelands of Australia. Notable for its spine-chilling, wolf-like howl, this dragon leaves its lair only when darkness falls.

ANATOMY
OF THE
DRAGON

Whether blazing across starry skies or slithering through murky waters, the spectacle of a dragon must be one of the most imposing sights in all of nature. Though the sheer variety found amongst dragonkind is of itself breathtaking, all species possess unique bodily features that set them apart from Earth's other creatures.

From all-seeing eyes to breath of fire or ice, the dragon's form and makeup is a source of constant wonder.

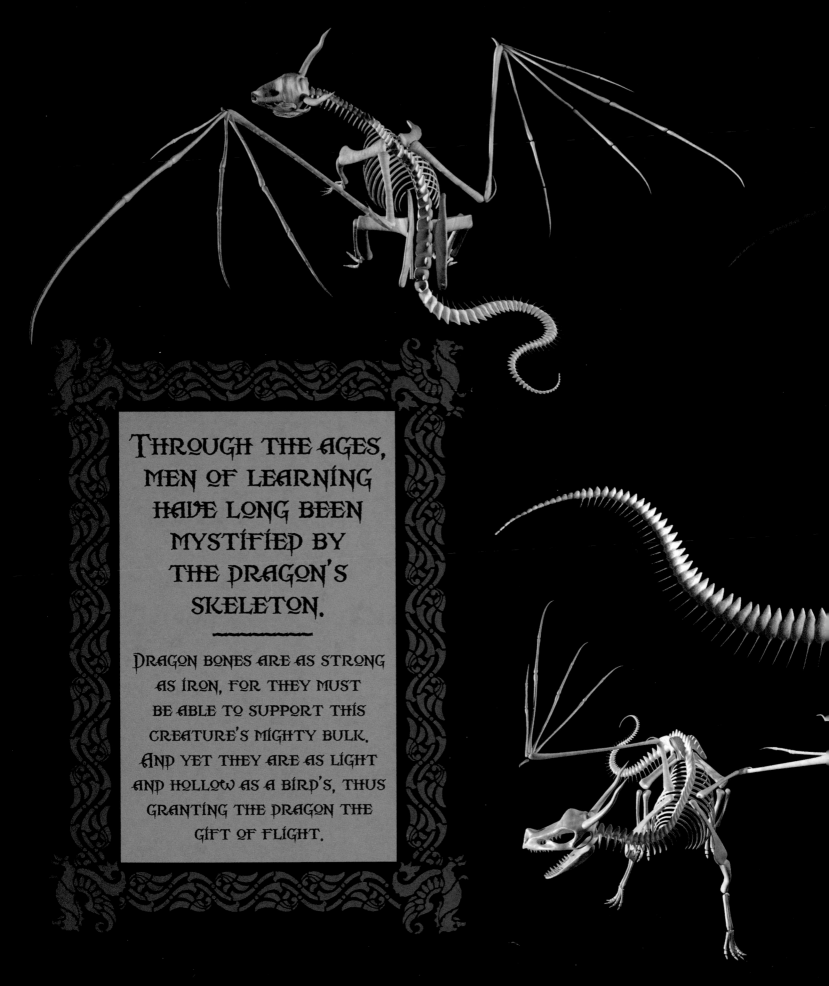

THROUGH THE AGES,
MEN OF LEARNING
HAVE LONG BEEN
MYSTIFIED BY
THE DRAGON'S
SKELETON.

DRAGON BONES ARE AS STRONG
AS IRON, FOR THEY MUST
BE ABLE TO SUPPORT THIS
CREATURE'S MIGHTY BULK.
AND YET THEY ARE AS LIGHT
AND HOLLOW AS A BIRD'S, THUS
GRANTING THE DRAGON THE
GIFT OF FLIGHT.

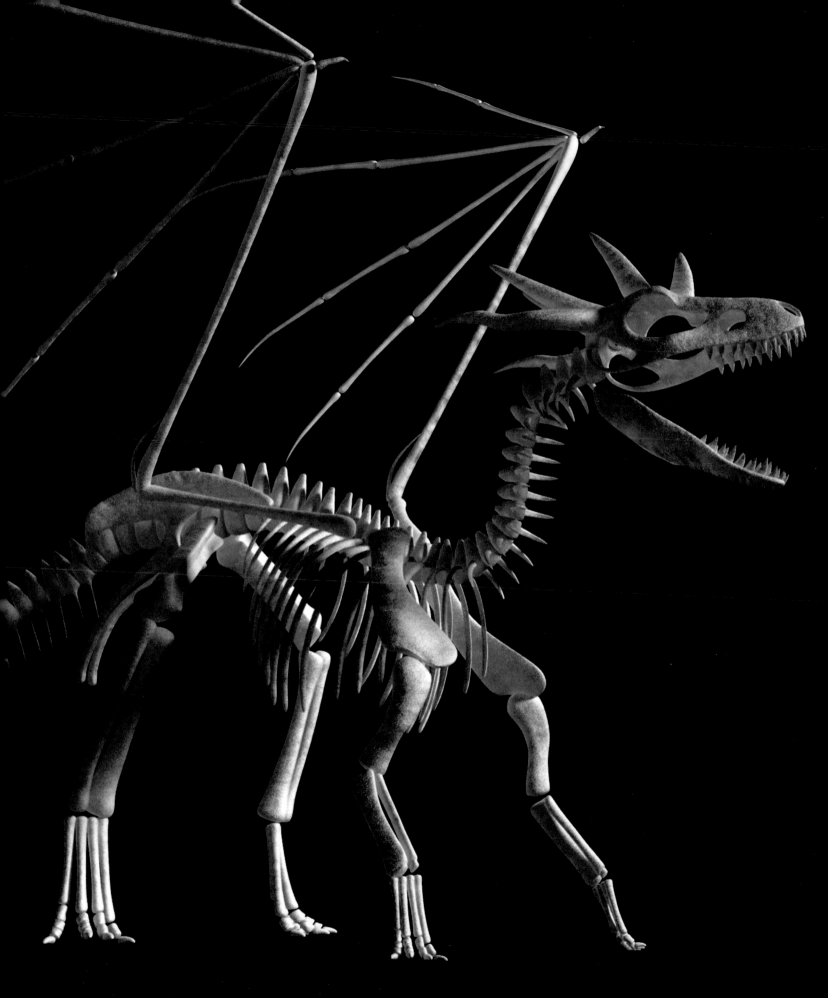

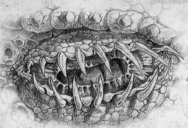

The protective thorn-like eyelashes of the SICKLE–CLAWED FOREST DRAGON.

Many water species possess a "second eye" – a translucent protective covering that allows these dragons to see underwater.

The uniquely-shaped eye pupil of the BLACK BOG DRAGON.

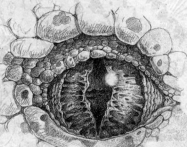

The vertical eye pupil of the TRIPLE–HORNED NIGHT DRAGON.

THE DRAGON'S SENSES
A STUDY OF SIGHT, HEARING & SMELL

MUCH HAS BEEN WRITTEN of the dragon's astonishing eyesight. Our own vision is so limited by comparison, that it is hard to imagine the world as beheld by dragons. They can observe a scene many miles away in perfect focus and possess the facility to see the full range of colours. What human eyes perceive as the sun's glare appears as sharply defined to the dragon. Naturally, their night vision is also exceptional.

Dragon eyes come in every imaginable hue from forest-green and sky-blue, to copper, bronze and burnished gold. It is a well-documented fact that it is very likely impossible, and certainly rather foolhardy, to hold the gaze of a dragon. Its stare is so penetrating and hypnotic, that it has the effect of placing the viewer in a trance from which they are unlikely to recover.

UNEARTHLY PERCEPTION

Although not in the same league as their eyesight, a dragon's hearing and sense of smell are not to be underestimated. Dragons can discern sounds well outside the human range, and have been known to respond to courting calls over fifty miles away. Similarly, dragons can detect and decode scents carried on the wind over vast distances. Although barely understood, it is evident that dragons also possess a sixth sense. A case in point would be their uncanny ability to seek out gold and precious stones hidden from view.

The Hook-beaked Mountain Dragon

This species is a fine example of how a dragon's remarkable senses work together to create a truly terrifying predator. The Hook-beaked Mountain Dragon's eyes can pinpoint victims from a distance of many miles, whilst its acute hearing and incredible sense of smell mean that it can also detect prey hidden from view.

Beware the glint in a dragon's eye:

Cold as ice to the liar,

Sharp as a knife to the knave,

Hard as iron to the greedy,

A burning flame to the brave.

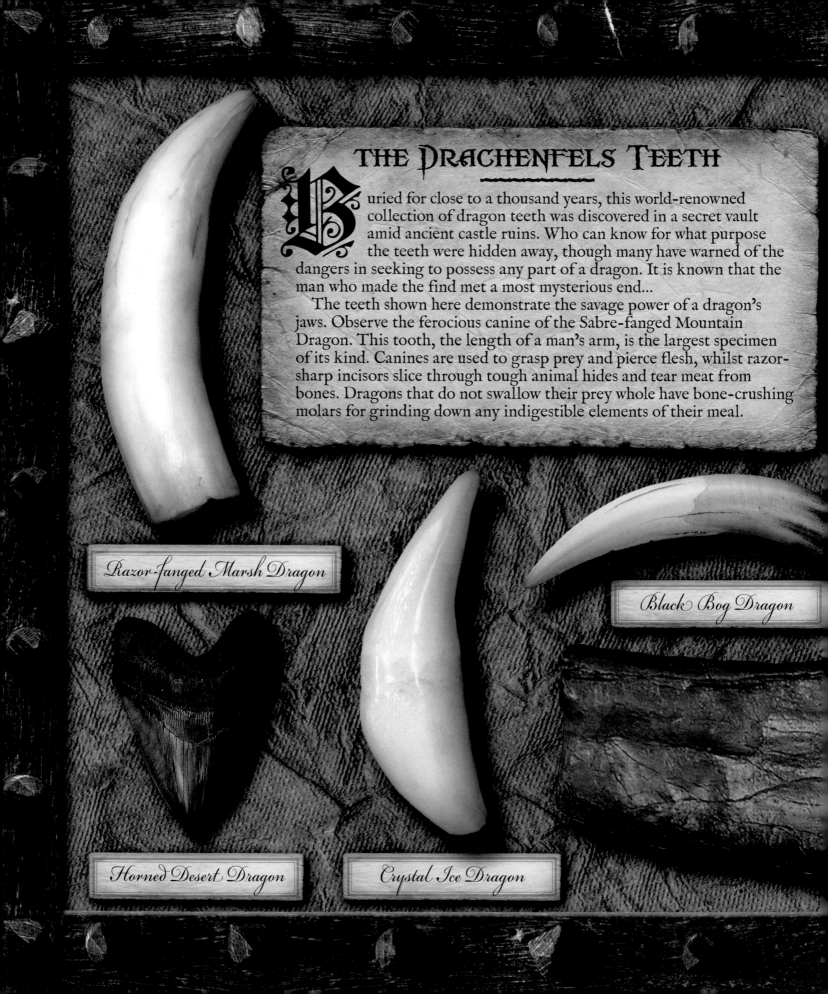

THE DRACHENFELS TEETH

Buried for close to a thousand years, this world-renowned collection of dragon teeth was discovered in a secret vault amid ancient castle ruins. Who can know for what purpose the teeth were hidden away, though many have warned of the dangers in seeking to possess any part of a dragon. It is known that the man who made the find met a most mysterious end...

The teeth shown here demonstrate the savage power of a dragon's jaws. Observe the ferocious canine of the Sabre-fanged Mountain Dragon. This tooth, the length of a man's arm, is the largest specimen of its kind. Canines are used to grasp prey and pierce flesh, whilst razor-sharp incisors slice through tough animal hides and tear meat from bones. Dragons that do not swallow their prey whole have bone-crushing molars for grinding down any indigestible elements of their meal.

Razor-fanged Marsh Dragon

Black Bog Dragon

Horned Desert Dragon

Crystal Ice Dragon

Arabian Sand Dragon

Himalayan Mountain Dragon

Sabre-fanged Mountain Dragon

Scales of the Wyrm Treasury

Drawn from the darkest corners of Europe, this collection of dragon scales is the pride of the Wyrm Treasury in Krakow, Poland. Legend holds that the scales will burst into flame should they ever be used to devise evil spells against dragonkind.

Scale samples of this size fall away from a dragon's body throughout its long life, though strangely they are almost never seen. From the scorching heat of the Vulcanian Fire Dragon to the frosty touch of the Black Ice Dragon, all dragon scale samples preserve the original body temperature of their hosts.

Siberian Frost Dragon

Burnished Water Dragon

Vulcanian Fire Dragon

Pygmy Forest Dragon

Five-clawed Serpent Dragon

Black Ice Dragon

Dragon Claws
A Study of Talons

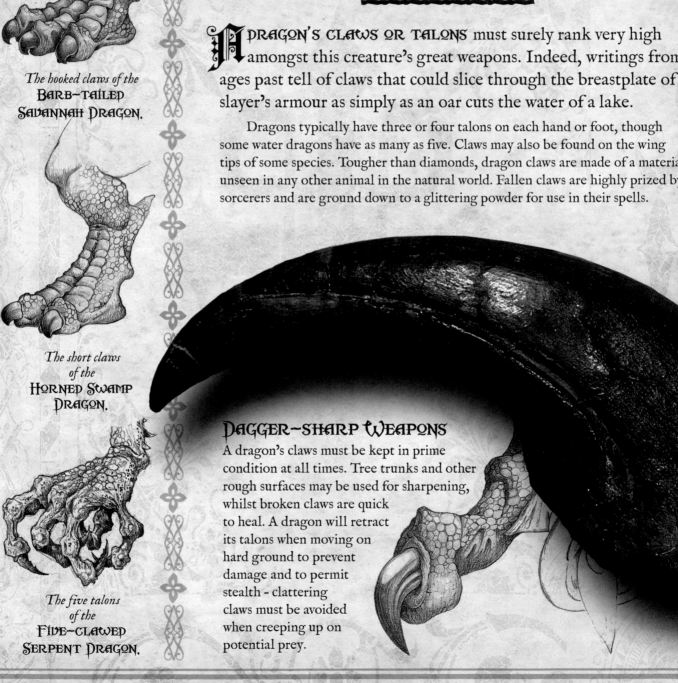

A DRAGON'S CLAWS OR TALONS must surely rank very high amongst this creature's great weapons. Indeed, writings from ages past tell of claws that could slice through the breastplate of a slayer's armour as simply as an oar cuts the water of a lake.

Dragons typically have three or four talons on each hand or foot, though some water dragons have as many as five. Claws may also be found on the wing tips of some species. Tougher than diamonds, dragon claws are made of a material unseen in any other animal in the natural world. Fallen claws are highly prized by sorcerers and are ground down to a glittering powder for use in their spells.

Dagger-Sharp Weapons

A dragon's claws must be kept in prime condition at all times. Tree trunks and other rough surfaces may be used for sharpening, whilst broken claws are quick to heal. A dragon will retract its talons when moving on hard ground to prevent damage and to permit stealth - clattering claws must be avoided when creeping up on potential prey.

The hooked claws of the **BARB-TAILED SAVANNAH DRAGON.**

The short claws of the **HORNED SWAMP DRAGON.**

The five talons of the **FIVE-CLAWED SERPENT DRAGON.**

THE SHARPENED TALONS OF THE
BLACK ICE DRAGON.

*A dragon's hands are both forceful and skilful. With a grip sufficient
to crush bones, their fingers are also incredibly nimble.*

Horns & Tails
Deadly Weapons in the Dragon's Armoury

A **dragon's horns or antlers** can prove quite devastating in attack, or indeed in self-defence. From the lethal spikes of the Bearded Mountain Dragon to the spiral antlers of many serpent dragons or the woody stumps of the Sickle-clawed Forest Dragon, a startling variety of horns and antlers are seen across the different species.

Horns are made of bone and are a permanent outgrowth of the dragon's skull. Since they never stop growing, they can reach quite staggering proportions. By contrast, antlers are shed yearly and are much sought after by sorcerers for their magical properties. Dragons use their horns and antlers to gore prey, and to win a mate in the breeding season when males often fight to the death. It goes without saying that the sight of two dragons locking horns in mortal combat is a terrifying spectacle.

The multiple horns of the
Red Prairie Dragon.

The spiked horns of the
Bearded Mountain Dragon.

The curved antlers of the
Burnished Water Dragon.

A horn belonging to the
Arabian Sand Dragon.

Terrible Tails

The tail is the dragon's secret weapon - a single lash may well prove deadly. Tails can be forked or arrow-tipped, spiked, and in some cases end in a bone-crushing club. Some species such as the Five-clawed Serpent Dragon can use their tails to literally squeeze the life out of a victim. However, in the case of this normally peaceful dragon, it should be stressed that this is almost always a defensive measure.

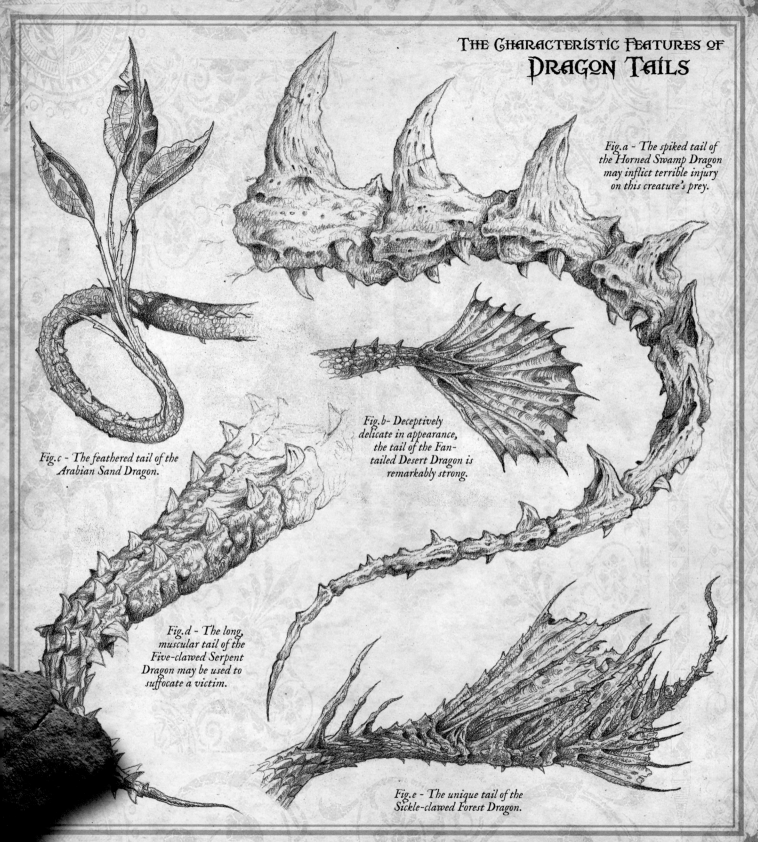

Fig.a - The spiked tail of the Horned Swamp Dragon may inflict terrible injury on this creature's prey.

Fig.c - The feathered tail of the Arabian Sand Dragon.

Fig.b - Deceptively delicate in appearance, the tail of the Fan-tailed Desert Dragon is remarkably strong.

Fig.d - The long, muscular tail of the Five-clawed Serpent Dragon may be used to suffocate a victim.

Fig.e - The unique tail of the Sickle-clawed Forest Dragon.

Wings of the Pike Collection

These incredibly rare wing fragments form part of the private collection of the world-renowned dragon hunter Dr Tiberius Pike. Quite how he chanced upon these beautifully preserved specimens remains a mystery, but a team of experts has confirmed their authenticity.

Laki Lava Dragon

Thought to be at least a hundred years old, this copper-red wing fragment belongs to the Laki Lava dragon of Iceland. Known to have survived the catastrophic Laki volcano of 1783, this species can tolerate incredible extremes of temperature.

The dragon wing is a thin yet amazingly robust structure. This particular wing sample is covered with a curious fire-resistant layer, the like of which has never before been seen in the natural world.

CRYSTAL ICE DRAGON

Preserved and mummified in Antarctic ice, this paper-thin wing fragment is believed to be over three thousand years old. The wing specimen was discovered next to the similarly aged fossilized thumb claw of the ferocious Black Ice Dragon. It is tempting to suppose these two dragons were engaged in mortal combat when they met their deaths.

Fossilized Thumb Claw of the Black Ice Dragon

DRAGON FIRE

Through the centuries many have tried and failed to explain the dragon's remarkable ability to breathe scorching flames of fire. Not all dragons are fire-breathers, but those that are possess a truly terrible weapon. A single blast nearly always results in instant death for the unfortunate victim. What then are we to make of this extraordinary phenomenon?

SOLVING THE RIDDLE

Experts now believe that the element phosphorus is the answer to this great mystery. All creatures need phosphorus to survive, but it is thought that chemical reactions within the dragon's body create the pure form, white phosphorus. Extremely flammable, white phosphorus will instantly ignite on exposure to air when cheek glands pass the element into the dragon's mouth. Glowing phosphorus traces found in the wake of dragon fire have provided tantalizing evidence to support this exciting theory.

The Way of the Dragon

Throughout the ages men have sought to uncover the secrets of dragonkind. It is widely held that dragons live anywhere between a thousand and ten thousand years, though it is impossible to know for certain. No dragon life has ever been studied in its entirety.

The observations on the following pages must be viewed as fragments of the whole. From birth to death, there is much in the dragon's way of life that remains cloaked in mystery. Wise is he who understands this must be so...

A hatchling of the
GOLDEN FIRE DRAGON.

The adolescent
GOLDEN FIRE DRAGON.

The mature
GOLDEN FIRE DRAGON.

AGES OF THE DRAGON
FROM BIRTH TO DEATH

SOME HAVE CLAIMED that most baby dragons remain in their eggs for three thousand years before hatching - a thousand in the ocean depths, a thousand on icy mountain peaks and a thousand warmed by the sun.

Depending on the species, a female adult lays anything between one and a hundred eggs. Eggs come in all shapes and sizes, and may be mistaken for exceptionally beautiful stones. It is believed that baby dragons make a high-pitched "singing" sound as the time of hatching approaches. Hatchlings emerge from their shells with the aid of an egg tooth at the end of their snouts, and at least one parent is present to greet them. If danger threatens, or in cases of extreme cold, the young may be carried inside their mother's mouth.

FROM HATCHLING TO DRAGON

Baby dragons resemble their parents in almost every respect, though their scales are soft, their horns undeveloped and their eyesight lacks the telescopic power of a mature adult. In the case of serpent species, ancient writings attest to wriggling hatchling snakes growing into mature dragons within a matter of minutes. However, for most the path to adulthood is believed to take several hundred years.

A DRAGON'S OLD AGE

As a dragon's final centuries approach, its body begins to show signs of aging. Elderly dragons become very gnarled in appearance, bright scales turn dull, and teeth and claws take on a yellow hue. As energy levels decrease and senses become less acute, these aged beasts are less inclined to travel large distances, and may become exceptionally bad tempered. However, despite the loss of physical prowess, ancient dragons have extraordinary wisdom and are revered throughout the dragon kingdom.

THE AGED FEATURES
OF THE OLDEST RECORDED
GOLDEN FIRE DRAGON.

Fig.a - Warts and bumps may appear, and eyes become sunken in appearance.

Fig.b - The tail has a ragged, moth-eaten appearance.

Fig.c - The wing claw is chipped and shows signs of yellowing.

THE SUMATRAN EGG COLLECTION

Very closely guarded on Sumatra, "The Island of Gold", the six dragon eggs of this curious collection are known to make a gentle humming sound when gathered together in one place.

1. ARABIAN SAND DRAGON
2. KRAKATOAN LAVA DRAGON
3. SUMATRAN WATER DRAGON
4. TRIPLE-HORNED NIGHT DRAGON
5. ANTARCTIC SNOW DRAGON
6. BEARDED MOUNTAIN DRAGON

1.

4.

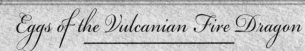

Eggs of the Vulcanian Fire Dragon

It is thought the eggs of this rare species incubate for several hundred years in red-hot liquid rock deep beneath the Earth's crust. Before hatching, the mother removes her eggs to the rim of an active volcano. The newborn dragons must bathe in bubbling lava for the first few weeks of their lives before they can adapt to cooler temperatures.

Food and Hunting

All dragons are meat-eaters, though many enjoy gnawing on vegetable matter too. The Copper-breasted Marsh Dragon of subtropical America is particularly fond of the blood berry plant, whilst the Long-snouted Water Dragon of southern Europe supplements its diet with the deadly mandrake root, poisonous to most animals.

The Dragon's Deathly Blows

Dragons employ a wide variety of methods to kill their prey. Many swoop down from on high with claws extended, and either carry off their prey or use ferocious jaws to consume a victim on the spot. Species living on open plains stalk their prey before bursting into a swift pursuit that is almost always over in a matter of seconds. Many wetland species lurk just beneath the surface of a swamp or marsh, rearing up to snatch a passing victim with razor-sharp fangs. Some species rely solely on fire-breathing to scorch their prey, whilst dragons living in snowy lands may breathe out blasts of icy air to stun a victim.

Super Senses

A few species employ more unusual hunting techniques. Emerging only in darkness, the Australian Triple-horned Night Dragon places an ear close to the ground, and is able to pinpoint prey such as the dingo from an astonishing distance. The Amazonian Water Dragon preys on the giant anaconda snake. Tiny hairs on the underside of this dragon's tail enable it to detect minute vibrations from the reptile at a distance of many miles.

Horned Desert Dragon

Horned Swamp Dragon

Burnished Water Dragon

Golden Fire Dragon

Great African Ram Dragon

Claws of the Drakon Expedition

Assembled by an eminent team of dragon specialists, this spectacular array of claws is the fruit of a long and arduous expedition involving five continents and some of the wildest places on Earth. The team crossed vast unpopulated stretches of forest, desert and ice, scaled treacherous mountain peaks and plunged deep into underground caverns to seek out these magnificent specimens. One life was lost, and one expert remains unaccounted for. Suffice to say, every claw in the Drakon collection has a tale to tell.

Claw Variety

These claws testify to the sheer variety found amongst dragonkind. Behold the curved barb of the Hook-clawed Mountain Dragon or the sharpened stake of the Flat-snouted Night Dragon. The claw shown here belonging to the Horned Desert Dragon is in fact a wing claw. This terrifying predator may call upon these talons found on each wing tip when engaged in aerial combat with rival dragons.

Hook-clawed Mountain Dragon

Flat-snouted Night Dragon

Barb-tailed Savannah Dragon

THE DRAGON LAIR
A STUDY OF CAVES, NESTS & BURROWS

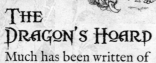

Sandstone rock shelters provide ideal lairs for desert dragons.

MORE THAN A NESTING SITE, the dragon's lair is a place of refuge. From labyrinthine caves to inaccessible cliff ledges, and from riverbank burrows to hollowed-out trees, dragon lairs are as diverse as dragon species. Beware the man who would hunt one out, for a dragon will guard its lair with its life!

YAWNING CAVES

Many dragons favour inky-black caves because they offer both space and solitude - the dragon is by its very nature aloof and secretive. Some species have been known to inhabit giant crystal caves, deep underground. Too hot for any other living creature, these rare glittering chambers are much sought after by treasure-loving dragons. Those species living in the frozen polar lands make their lairs in ice and glacier caves. Although most dragons settle in one lair for life, ice dragons need to be adaptable as glacier caves can never be a permanent home.

NESTS, BURROWS AND HOLES

Some mountain dragons make their nests high up on remote and rugged cliffs. They choose wild and windy areas where updrafts help them to gain height and reach their nests whilst carrying heavy prey. Smaller species such as woodland dragons make nests in treetops, or in hollowed-out tree trunks. Dragons found on open plains may scratch a hole in the ground to hold their nests. Some species such as the Black Dwarf Dragon burrow underground, creating elaborate interconnecting tunnels, whilst many water species dig simple holes in riverbanks.

THE DRAGON'S HOARD

Much has been written of the dragon's love of treasure, although some dragons are more adept than others in the pursuit of precious gems. Almost all lairs will contain a cache of stones, be it made up of sparkling sapphires or gleaming pebbles. Those humans who risk their lives in pursuit of the dragon's hoard will very likely feel frustration when they encounter only the latter.

This precious gold nugget once belonged to an Arabian Sand Dragon.

Dragons living in snowy lands seek refuge in ice caves.

*Spacious caves are much sought-after
by the larger mountain species.*

*A hollow tree trunk provides the
perfect lair for small woodland species.*

To he who seeks the dragon's lair
And prizes rich beyond compare,
Rubies red and glittering gold,
Pray heed these words of ages old:

———

Should such treasures fill
your purse,
Beware the power of a
dragon's curse!

DRACHENFELS

High up on jagged rocks overlooking the German Rhineland lie ancient castle ruins. Legend holds it was here that Siegfried slew the dragon Fafnir. Afterwards, Siegfried roasted the beast's heart and drank its blood. This gave him the ability to understand the speech of birds.

Dragons are strangely drawn to this mystical site known as Drachenfels. Few people have seen these creatures - hiding in their lairs by day, the dragons emerge only under cover of darkness. However, on a still moonlit night, some say you may hear the soft beat of a wing, or catch a glimpse of shadowy forms circling the craggy rocks.

Legend
and Lore

Dragons have always stalked this world. Ancient writings and legends handed down by our ancestors tell of many encounters with these fearsome creatures – horrifying accounts of monstrous beasts, tales of courage and valour, stories of magic and mystery.

In the field of dragon studies, this creature's powerful magic remains as puzzling today as it ever was. To those who seek to know the dragon, pay heed to the legends and lore of yesteryear – for there is much for us to learn.

Magic and Mystery
Enchantment and Sorcery

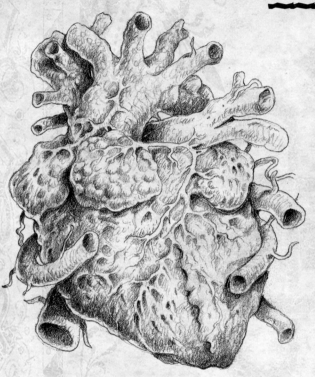

The enormous heart of the Bearded Mountain Dragon.

THROUGH THE CENTURIES, sorcerers and alchemists have long desired to harness the dragon's powerful magic for their own purposes. Many parts of the dragon are known to possess magical properties, though there is much that remains shrouded in mystery. Great care is needed in dealing with dragon parts, for although their magic may be put to good use, so too can it cause terrible harm in the wrong hands.

The Heart

There are those who say a dragon's soul resides in its heart. Dragon slayers from ages past were known to have plucked out a victim's heart and consumed it, for they believed this would impart the gift of prophecy.

Blood

Perhaps the most powerful part of a dragon is its blood. Wizards will go to great lengths to secure this potent substance for their spell casting, though many have failed to appreciate its full force. Spells that use dragon blood in the wrong combinations or amounts can bring about catastrophic consequences.

Bones

The bones of fallen dragons are much sought after for their healing qualities. Ground down to a fine powder, they are used in spells to treat a range of ailments from the common cold to broken bones.

A femur bone from the rear limb of the Golden Fire Dragon.

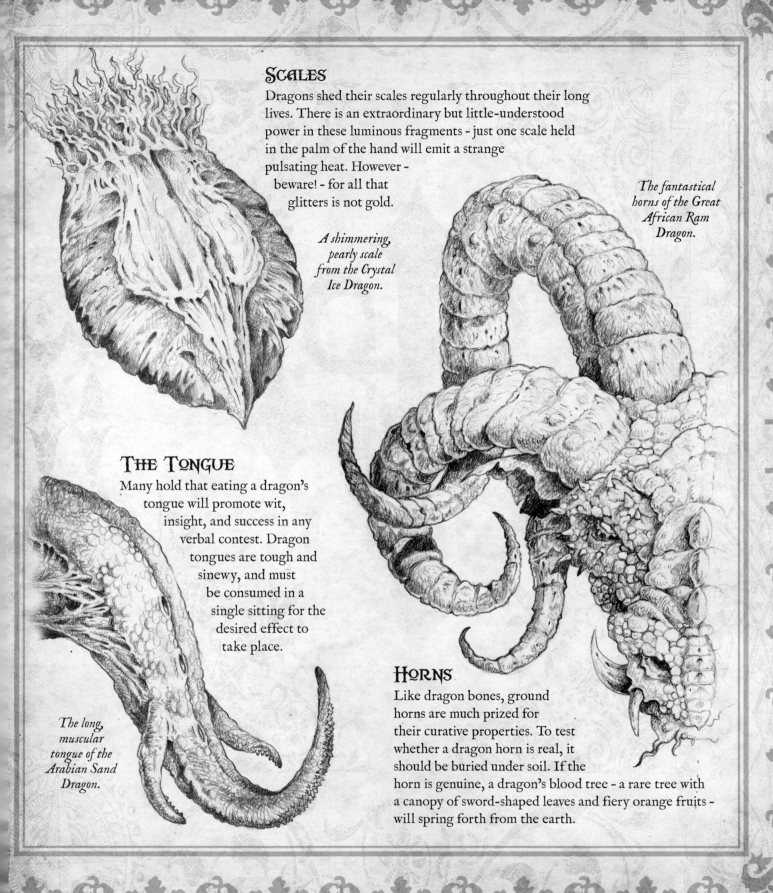

SCALES

Dragons shed their scales regularly throughout their long lives. There is an extraordinary but little-understood power in these luminous fragments - just one scale held in the palm of the hand will emit a strange pulsating heat. However - beware! - for all that glitters is not gold.

A shimmering, pearly scale from the Crystal Ice Dragon.

The fantastical horns of the Great African Ram Dragon.

THE TONGUE

Many hold that eating a dragon's tongue will promote wit, insight, and success in any verbal contest. Dragon tongues are tough and sinewy, and must be consumed in a single sitting for the desired effect to take place.

The long, muscular tongue of the Arabian Sand Dragon.

HORNS

Like dragon bones, ground horns are much prized for their curative properties. To test whether a dragon horn is real, it should be buried under soil. If the horn is genuine, a dragon's blood tree - a rare tree with a canopy of sword-shaped leaves and fiery orange fruits - will spring forth from the earth.

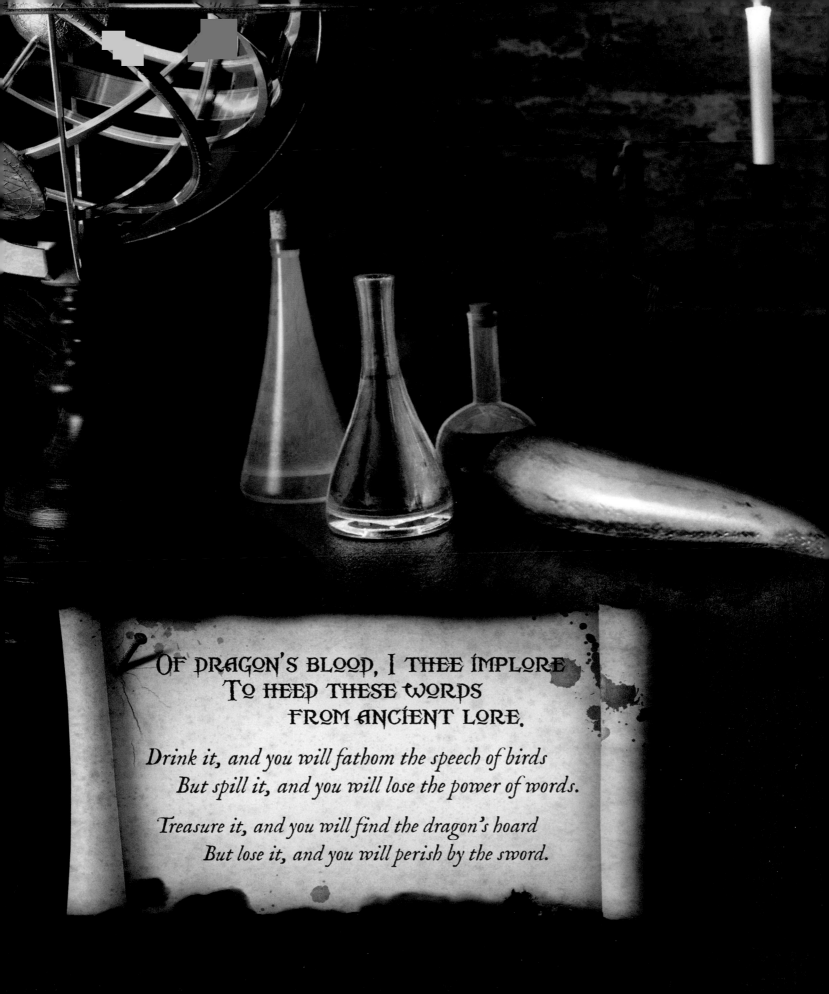

OF DRAGON'S BLOOD, I THEE IMPLORE
TO HEED THESE WORDS
FROM ANCIENT LORE.

Drink it, and you will fathom the speech of birds
But spill it, and you will lose the power of words.

Treasure it, and you will find the dragon's hoard
But lose it, and you will perish by the sword.

THE DRAGON'S PEARL

Only the very oldest dragons possess a precious pearl of wisdom. Formed at the beginning of time, these ancient gems are thought to contain fragments of moon substance, such that they gleam in darkness. Many believe these stones contain the wisdom of the sun, the moon and the stars. He who chances upon a dragon's pearl will be wise indeed...

Dragon Legends
Tales from Yesteryear

Many of the dragons that haunted our ancestors still roam our world today, though some species have become extinct. Writings tell of magnificent winged beasts and monstrous scaled serpents; of fire-breathing harbingers of disaster, and dragons of wisdom and knowledge. Those who wish to further their knowledge of the dragon should be careful to acquaint themselves with those creatures that have gone before.

O-gon-cho, The Golden Dragon Bird

The people of Kyoto in Japan were once plagued by the O-gon-cho, a great white dragon living in a deep, murky lake. Every fifty years the dragon transformed into a golden songbird with glowing yellow feathers, and rose to the skies. But despite its beauty, the people dreaded seeing or hearing the O-gon-cho. Its spine-chilling howl tore through the land, and always foretold famine or disease.

Mother Dragon

A very long time ago an old woman was walking along a great river. There she came across five beautiful stones lying hidden in grass, and picking them up took them back to her home. They were so exquisite that she gazed at them many times a day. One night there was a terrible storm. As jagged lightning tore the sky and thunder cracked overhead, the stones broke open and out crawled five baby dragons - for the stones were in fact dragon eggs. Quickly the old lady picked up the serpent-like hatchlings, and hurried back to the river where she released them. So grateful were the dragons that lived there for the return of their young, that they gave the woman the ability to see the future. Wise beyond telling, she became known throughout the land as Mother Dragon.

THE WAWEL DRAGON OF KRAKOW

Many centuries ago in Poland, there lived an enormous fire-breathing dragon. Occupying a deep, black cave on Wawel Hill, it would terrorize the nearby village, destroying land, consuming livestock, and preying on young women. Many attempted to kill this fearsome beast, but were scorched to death by its breath. One day a poor shoemaker's apprentice named Krakus fed a lamb with sulphur and placed it outside the dragon's cave. After consuming the lamb, the beast was tortured by a terrible fire in its belly.

It drank and drank from the nearby Vistula river, but its thirst could not be quenched. Continuing to drink, the dragon swelled terribly until it suddenly burst. There was much rejoicing at the dragon's death, and Krakus was made ruler of the village. Under his wise leadership the city of Krakow grew up around the hill.

DRAGON SLAYERS

Epic Tales of Courage and Adventure

Dragons are much revered in today's world, but it was not always so. In ages past, these majestic beasts were frequently misunderstood and provoked into acts of fury. Many a man has taken up arms against the dragon but only a very few have emerged victorious. The dragon slayer's tale is one of wit and bravery pitted against the brute strength of nature's mightiest creature...

WHO ARE THE MEN WHO DARE TO
TAKE THE NAME OF DRAGON SLAYER?
THEIR TALES ARE WRITTEN IN BLOOD
AND LIVE ON FOREVER MORE.

Hidden away in a secret underground vault, the astonishing relics displayed here immortalize some of their heroic battles. Only rarely have human eyes dared gaze upon these objects though, for it is said the wrath of slain dragons lives on in them…

SAINT GEORGE'S SPEAR

This bloodied spear tip comes from the very weapon that Saint George used to battle with the swamp-dwelling dragon of Silene in Libya. This fearsome beast demanded the daily sacrifice of a young woman and Saint George was determined to slay it. Observe how the spear's iron tip has been scratched and damaged - the dragon's scales were harder than diamonds and countless blows from George's spear came to nothing. The brave warrior was finally able to slay this terrible foe when he plunged his spear deep into a tiny patch of exposed skin beneath the dragon's wing.

THE
SCALE OF FAFNIR

The glittering scale you see before you belonged to none other than Fafnir, a dragon that guarded a hoard of gold many hundreds of years ago. Sigurd, a Norse hero, set out to slay this dreadful beast, and had a sword made so sharp it could slice through iron. He then hid himself in a shallow pit, and waited near the dragon's lair. In time the enormous creature passed over Sigurd's hiding place, and the hero was able to drive his sword into its underbelly. He then cut out the dragon's heart and drank its blood.

Still warm to the touch, this scale emits an eerie red glow, and is said to lightly quiver if held in the hand.

THE
BEOWULF TOOTH

This dagger-like tooth is over a thousand years old, and belonged to the frightful dragon that spread terror during the reign of the Anglo-Saxon king, Beowulf. When a goblet was stolen from the dragon's glittering hoard, the enraged beast set about scorching the land with its fiery breath. The heroic Beowulf dared to take on this foe, but as he struck the dragon's head, the beast plunged its poisonous fangs into the king's neck. The mortally wounded Beowulf managed to stagger up to slay the dragon by thrusting his sword deep into its heart, before himself falling dead to the ground.

As sharp as the day it was plucked from the slain dragon's jaws, legend holds this tooth will draw blood from any who touch it...

What man would seek
       the dragon's lair
Or meet the dragon's
          fearsome stare?

And who would face
       a dragon's jaws,
His sharpened teeth,
          his savage claws?

Which man would risk
       a dragon's breath –
The fiery heat
          of certain death?

Or seek to find
       the dragon's pearl
And all the knowledge
          in the world?

That man is brave,
          I know it well
But is he wise?
          Pray who can tell?